DONALD HAS A DIFFICULTY
PETER F. NEUMEYER & EDWARD GOREY

Harry N. Abrams, Inc., Publishers

CURR
P2
J445
Or
2004

Dedicated to the haunting memory of Edward Gorey
—P.F.N.

Another time Donald had a splinter.

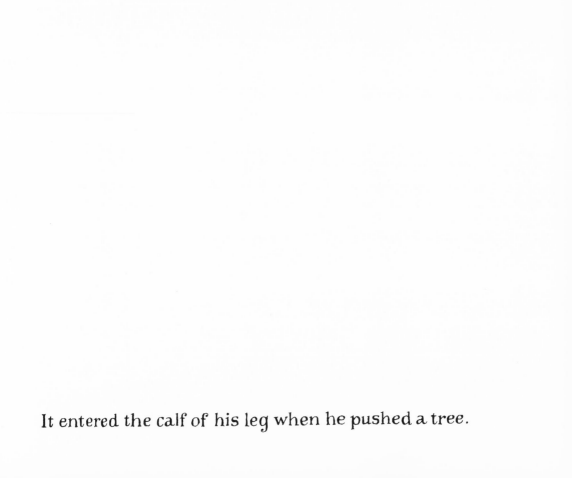

It entered the calf of his leg when he pushed a tree.

Donald's mother felt his hurt keenly. She prepared to remove the splinter from Donald's calf.

She arranged a tray with instruments.

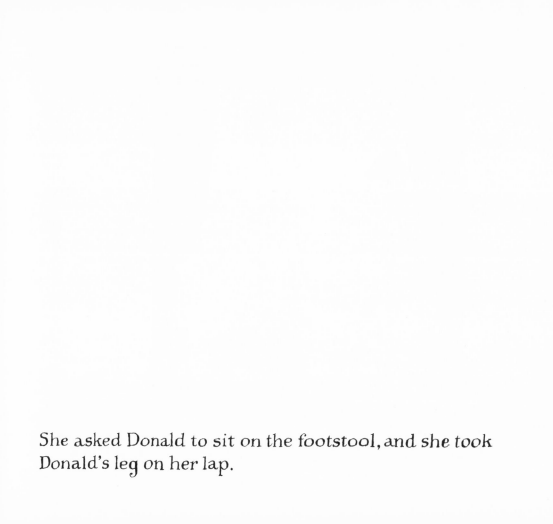

She asked Donald to sit on the footstool, and she took Donald's leg on her lap.

She told Donald to think of other things

of markets

of battles

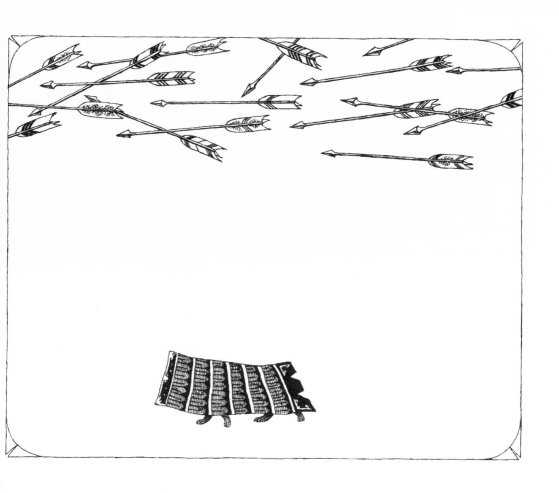

of strings

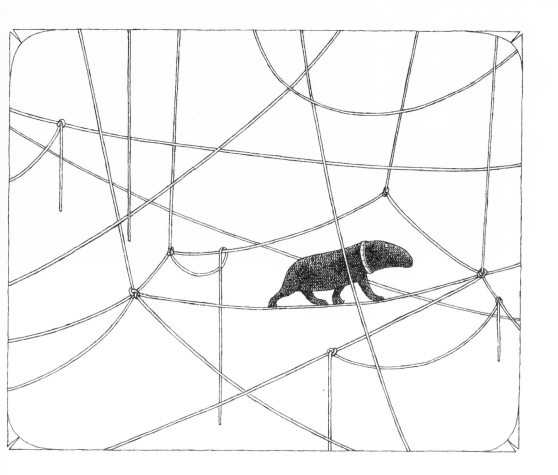

and with very good light she worked to remove the
splinter with

a needle

tweezers.

Donald's mother had success.
She showed the splinter to Donald.

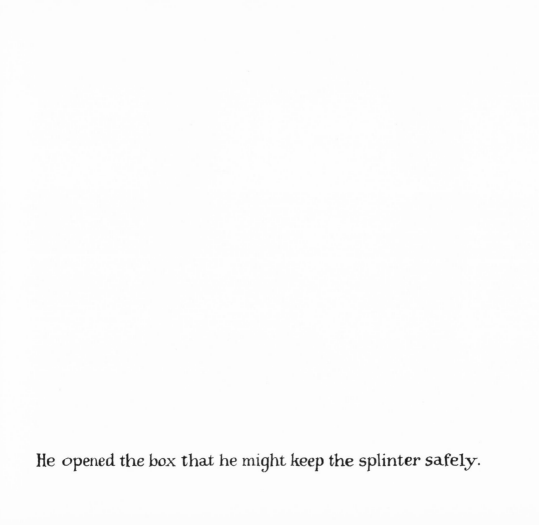

He opened the box that he might keep the splinter safely.

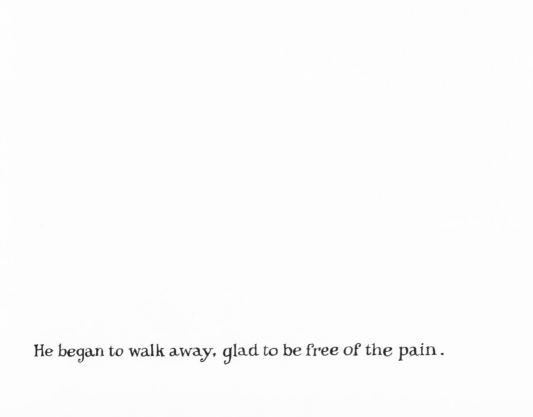

He began to walk away, glad to be free of the pain.

Donald's mother called him back.
'We must put alcohol on the wound,' she said.

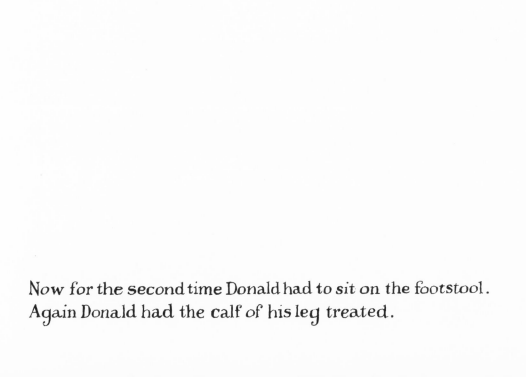

Now for the second time Donald had to sit on the footstool.
Again Donald had the calf of his leg treated.

He forgot to think of markets, battles, strings.
When Donald's mother touched the wound with cotton
dipped in alcohol, Donald shouted loudly, 'Oh my, how that hurts!'

Donald's mother then got pillows and made Donald comfortable in a deep chair.

'Neither the needle nor the tweezers hurt,' she said gently. 'Isn't it strange how it hurt only when we put alcohol on the wound?'

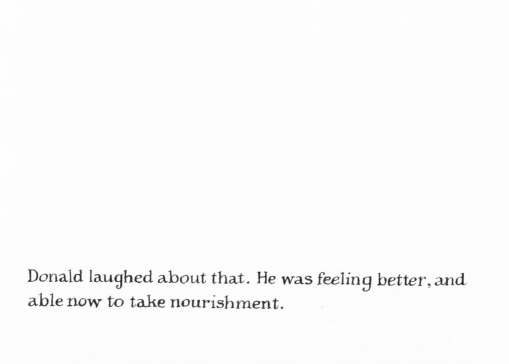

Donald laughed about that. He was feeling better, and able now to take nourishment.

The Saga of Donald Continues

"I've never had anything to do with the author of a book I was illustrating before," Edward Gorey wrote me in 1968. Nonetheless, in 1968 and 1969, Gorey and I worked closely together, creating three books—*Donald and the . . .* (1969), *Donald Has a Difficulty* (1970), and *Why We Have Day and Night* (1970). During the years of our collaboration, Ted shuttled between New York and Cape Cod. I was teaching at Harvard and living in Medford, Massachusetts. Although I stayed with Ted on the Cape, and he stayed with us in Medford, we did a great deal of our planning by way of long phone calls and the postal service, and there remain with me literally hundreds of pages of Ted's letters. I would always wait expectantly for these letters because most were enclosed in beautiful, Goreyesquely painted envelopes, some of these being preliminary drafts for a book we were working on. On one, there is a lovely little painting of Donald hanging on to an umbrella, windblown into future adventures. Occasionally there would be a postcard—merely a piece of dental floss scotch-taped to the card, or an anchovy label or theater stub. Heaven only knows what the mailman thought.

The "Donald" stories were actually vaguely thought to go on forever, Gorey writing me at one point, "I have just purchased lots of pristine new file folders. They await such things as . . . revised Donalds, new Donalds, new Lionels [another series], what else?" Another time, he wrote that "[M]y mind's eye sees a shelf of Neumeyer/Gorey works. Will Harvard have a room devoted to our memorabilia? It had better."

For *Donald Has a Difficulty*, Gorey's idea was first to publish an edition of 500 with the Fantod Press, his personal imprint, and then, as he jokingly wrote, "it's our full colour epic with a tiny note . . . to the effect that it's a revised second edition."

Gorey himself overflowed with ideas for the projected series: *Donald's Dream* and *Donald Makes a List*, a beautifully worked out and somewhat autobiographical tale in which Donald carefully wipes his pen and goes to work drawing "all sorts of wild, poetic, baroque things . . . to have no point except [their] own existence." This Donald was inspired by Jorge Luis Borges's curious tale of "The Analytical Language of John Wilkins," which divides all animals into categories such as "(a) those that belong to the emperor, (b) embalmed ones, (c) those that are trained, . . . etc." and which we had just read together. Gorey also suggested a "night-piece for Donald done in absolutely simple unshaded line . . . ," a *Donald's Alphabet*, and "a Donald . . . done in silhouette like some of the 19th century German things . . ." The unending series never came to be, though shortly before his death, Ted once again returned to Donald. How far he got, only perusal of his vast legacy of papers would show.

Ted slipped away, a good, kind man of a very specific genius. As I roam my bookshelves today, I can reconstruct some of the enthusiasms of that most generous of friends—a few of the many books he insisted on sending me so we could talk about them: Cyril Connoly's *The Unquiet Grave* and *The Rock Pool;* four volumes of Haiku, translated by Roland Blyth; L. H. Myers's *The Near and the Far;* Raymond Queneau's *The Blue Flowers* and *Exercises in Style;* Flann O'Brian's *The Best of Myles na Gopaleen;* Rayner Heppenstall's *The Lesser Infortune; The Journal of Jules Renard* (edited and translated by Louise Bogan and Elizabeth Roget); *Easy Poems, Books One and Two*, also with notes by Roland Blyth; and a beautiful giant Abrams book on Pisanello—and many, many more.

Heaven would be to resume those conversations.

Library of Congress Cataloging-in-Publication Data

Neumeyer, Peter F.,
Donald has a difficulty / Peter F. Neumeyer ; drawings by Edward
Gorey.
p. cm.
Summary: Donald encounters a difficulty when a splinter enters the calf
of his leg.
ISBN 0-8109-4835-4
[1. Wounds and injuries—Fiction.] I. Gorey, Edward, 1925– ill. II. Title.

PZ7.N445Dr 2004
[E]—dc22
2003013909

Printed and bound in China
10 9 8 7 6 5 4 3 2 1

Harry N. Abrams, Inc.
100 Fifth Avenue, New York, NY 10011
www.abramsbooks.com

Abrams is a subsidiary of

LA MARTINIÈRE
G R O U P E

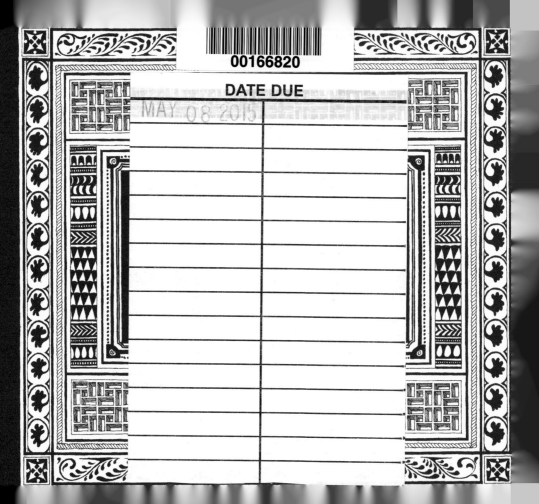